STACH

SHOUTYKID is a great book... If you like *Diary of a Wimpy Kid* or *Tom Gates* you will like this book... it's really funny and it made me laugh.
Isaac, age 8

Awesome, epic, funny and entertaining. I love the way the book is written in the form of letters and emails and texts. I hope that the author writes lots more adventures for Harry.
William, age 9

Totally awesome... the trials of *Harry Riddles's* life are laugh-out-loud funny. I could not stop laughing. Go out and grab a copy, you won't be disappointed.

Leia, age 10

Amazingly funny.

Rohan, age 8

Amazing and funny, I loved it! Harry Riddles is a great character... He does silly things but is pretty smart.

Frank, age 8

SHOUTYKID

How Harry Riddles
Totally Went Wild

SHOUTYKID

HOW Harry Riddles
Totally Went Wild

by SIMON
MAYLE

Illustrated by Nikalas Catlow

HarperCollins *Children's Books*

First published in Great Britain by HarperCollins *Children's Books* 2016
HarperCollins *Children's Books* is a division of HarperCollins*Publishers* Ltd,
HarperCollins *Publishers*
1 London Bridge Street
London SE1 9GF

The HarperCollins *Children's Books* website address is
www.harpercollins.co.uk

1

SHOUTYKID – HOW HARRY RIDDLES
TOTALLY WENT WILD
Text copyright © Simon Mayle 2016
Illustrations © Nikalas Catlow 2016

Simon Mayle and Nikalas Catlow assert the moral right to be
identified as the author and illustrator of this work.

ISBN 978-0-00-815888-0
Printed and bound in England by
Clays Ltd, St Ives plc

MIX
Paper from
responsible sources
FSC www.fsc.org **FSC™ C007454**

For Mum. Happy Birthday xx

From Harry Riddles **to** Charley Riddles
Subject: Half term
1 February 18:43 GMT

Dear Cuz –

At breakfast this morning my dad told me him and my mum have finally found something they think I'm gonna LOVE to do over half term.

Well, I didn't say anything, because I knew *exactly* what I wanted to do over this half term: play the new *World of Zombies* game, 'Carpocalypse Now: Ride of the Zombies', and see if I can become a Major

League Gamer. But I hadn't told them about the MLG plan, so I kept my mouth shut and hoped maybe they'd talk about something else (like Charlotte's e-NORMOUS phone bill).

But that didn't work, cos my sister starts cackling like the evil witch she is, so I go, "What's so funny, Charlotte?" and she says, "Two words for you, Harry. Pony Club – remember?"

Well, basically, that was the last time Mum and Dad found something they thought I'd love to do. And I didn't like that day at all. But my dad goes, "This isn't going to be like Pony Club! Getting stung on your mouth, your ear, and then having those horrible horse flies crawl down the back of your pants? Any kid would fall off a horse after that! But this thing your mum and me want you to think about doing? Could be *so*

great for you, Harry! And such a fun thing to do
– right, Rita?"

So I look up at my mum and she says, "I just
wish I could have done something like this when

I was your age!" And before I can ask what this great thing might be, my dad dumps a big colour brochure down in front of me. "Take a look at this!" he says. "You're gonna *love* this, Harry!"

So I look at the cover. I see a kid in a climbing hat, wearing a harness, swinging on a rope. My sister grabs it and goes, "You want to send Harry to Whippington Hall? He'll *hate* that place! It'll be like going to a *gulag* for a kid like him!"

Well, I googled gulag and if this place is anything like *that* nightmare, I'm NOT going.

Yr cousin,

Harry

From Charley **to** Harry
Subject: Gulags 4 kids
1 February 12:05 MST

Cuz –

Don't listen to your stupid sister. I went
to Kidz Camp when I was your age. It was
GREAT! You know what the best bit was? NO
PARENTS!

Charley

From Harry **to** Charley
1 February 19:17 GMT

Yeah, but I like my parents (most of the time).
Plus, this camp isn't out in California where you

live; it's over in Devon, which is *not* going to be as much fun – unless you want to stay wet and cold for, like, four days.

From Charley **to** Harry
1 February 12:22 MST

Cuz –

EVERYBODY loves going to camp. It's all part of becoming a BIG MAN. You should do it.

From Harry **to** Charley
1 February 19:25 GMT

Yeah, but I don't need to go to camp to become a big man. I can do that at home. Plus, staying here will be a LOT cheaper and my dad said we're going to have to live on a budget now that Charlotte's phone bill has nearly bankrupted us. But maybe her being an idiot on her phone in France and Facebooking everybody all the time is a *good* thing. Maybe that's just the excuse I need to get out of going to camp? Tell Pups to save the money, not spend it on me doing something I'm gonna HATE. What do you think? Good idea?

Harry

From Charley **to** Harry
1 February 12:31 MST

Not gonna work.

From Harry **to** Charley
1 February 19:36 GMT

You're right. Grandma just called and told Mum
she wants to pay for me to go. As an early
birthday treat kind of thing. But I don't know
where Grandma got her early birthday treat
ideas from, cos activity camp is definitely *not* on
my birthday list.

Birthday List!!!

1) Go to the World of Zombies
eSports tournament in London and
become a Major League Gamer!!!
2) Get loads more video games.
3) Get rid of Charlotte.

From Charley **to** Harry
1 February 12:39 MST

Cuz –

Just GO! It'll be really FUN!!

_____

From Harry **to** Charley
1 February 19:41 GMT

Yeah, but I don't think it's for me.

_____

From Charley **to** Harry
1 February 12:43 MST

Why not?

From Harry **to** Charley
1 February 19:44 GMT

Cos.

———————————

From Charley **to** Harry
1 February 12:46 MST

Cos what, you little Smurf?

———————————

From Harry **to** Charley
1 February 19:50 GMT

Cos what happens if I go and everybody finds out I
get really scared of the dark?

CHAPTER TWO
THE GREAT OUTDOORS

From Harry **to** Charley
Subject: Dad
5 February 19:04 GMT

That's it. I am so DOOOOOOOOOOMED!!!

From Charley **to** Harry
5 February 12:06 MST

What r u talking about, Harry?

From Harry **to** Charley
5 February 19:08 GMT

Activity camp.

From Charley **to** Harry
5 February 12:10 MST

What about it?

From Harry **to** Charley
5 February 19:15 GMT

OK, so basically, I'm up in my room playing the last quarter of this epic one v one death match with this kid called darkassassin300. Which, if I win, gets me an invite to join his elite HandControllerz gamer team. And these MLG guys are going all the way up to Wembley next month to play in this big *World of Zombies* eSports tournament. So this game is probably *the* most important video game of my WHOLE gaming life.

But my dad comes in my room and he won't leave until I've read his brochure, cos he says Mr Forbes needs to know if I'm going to camp or not. So I tell darkassassin300 I have to go and do something with my dad for, like, the next ten minutes, can we take a short break? And he's like, "Oh, sure, we can take a break if you want to get *killed*! But this is a one v one *death match*, brah! And winner takes all!"

But my dad won't leave till I've looked at the brochure. So I open it. First line I read is, "There's something special about the great outdoors!" And right then, I hear this enormous *BAAAAAANG!!!* from outside my bedroom window. Two seconds later there's this huge *ZAAAAAAAAAP!!!* And a bolt of lightning hits our power line. Next, all the lights go out. Then my Xbox crashes. Then the dog runs under my bed and starts howling, cos he's, like,

scared the world's ending. Then my phone pings!
Then I get this text from 300 saying I rage quit, cos
I was losing!

Well, if that isn't a sign I shouldn't be spending my half term at some stupid activity camp, I don't know what is.

From Charley **to** Harry
5 February 12:17 MST

So u said no?

From Harry **to** Charley
5 February 19:18 GMT

No.

From Charley **to** Harry
5 February 12:20 MST

U said yes?

_____

From Harry **to** Charley
5 February 19:21 GMT

Uh-huh.

_____

From Charley **to** Harry
5 February 12:23 MST

How come?

From Harry **to** Charley
5 February 19:25 GMT

Cos after my dad fixes all the fuses, he comes back up to my room and he goes, "What do you think, Harry? You want to go?" I tell him I think I'm better off staying at home. So he starts shrugging and coughing and making all these funny faces, so I go, "What?" And he tells me how he saw Jessica's mum at school and she said if I wasn't going, at least Jessica could spend some time writing some new songs with Kevin, cos they are both *super* excited to be going to camp.

From Charley **to** Harry
5 February 12:41 MST

Is this that band kid, who was after your girl?

From Harry **to** Charley
5 February 19:44 GMT

Yeah. He still likes her. Even though he knows me and her are officially going out.

From Charley **to** Harry
5 February 12:47 MST

So what did you say?

From Harry **to** Charley
5 February 19:51 GMT

I said, "Well, if Kevin's going, maybe I should go too." And my dad goes, "Great! I'll tell Mr Forbes!" And before I can change my mind, he's mailed

Forbes and now I'm going (which, BTW, is pretty scary).

From Charley **to** Harry
5 February 12:53 MST

Squid –

You're gonna have a GREAT time. Don't worry. It'll be really cool.

From Harry **to** Charley
5 February 19:55 GMT

Hmm.

CHAPTER THREE
THE DARK ARTS

From Harry **to** Paul McKenna
Subject: The Dark Arts
8 February 19:20 GMT

Dear Paul McKenna, world-famous hypnotist and
TV personality, hi there!

I'm going away to activity camp for half term, but
I know when I get there I'm going to have a big
problem with this kid Ed Bigstock.

At the weekend my friend Bulmer had a birthday party
and invited me and ten other kids to his farm for a
sleepover and BB gun shoot-out, which, BTW, was really
good fun, cos basically I owned Bigstock at Lone Wolf.

Anyway, after we finish our last battle we go inside
to eat, and me and Bigstock get in this big fight,
cos he steals my last slice of pizza as payback for

me beating him at battles in the barn.

So then we go in the front room to watch this video and we put our sleeping bags out on the floor, but after all that sneaking around outside I'm super tired, so I fall asleep and when I wake up it's a LOT later. And there's NO lights on. And I don't like the dark, so this is, like, a really big deal for me.

But I think, OK, OK, I'll just go find a light and then everything will be cool (maybe). So I get out of my sleeping bag and I creep over to the door. But just as I reach for the light switch, my foot kicks this thing that's big and round like a bowling ball.

Only it's NOT a bowling ball – it's Ed Bigstock's HEAD. And he wakes up and goes NUTS. So I jump back and

I stamp on this *other* kid's hand. And this kid (his name's Kevin), he goes nuts, so now I got both Bigstock *and* Kevin yelling at me cos they think I must be some kind of BURGLAR.

Well that woke the whole house up, and next thing I know Mr Bulmer comes charging into the room in his underwear, holding a cricket bat, telling us kids not to worry, he's a black belt in karate, but where's the burglar gone?

So I have to explain to Mr Bulmer that there is no
burglar, there's only me. And I was just trying to
find the bathroom (I didn't mention the light bit).
Luckily, Bulmer's dad said we should probably
leave the light on for the rest of the night, so that
worked out OK for me. But Bigstock now thinks
I kicked him in the head as payback for him
stealing my last slice of pizza and as soon as we
are alone at camp he's going to KILL ME. Which is
kind of why I need your help.

Can you teach me how to control people's thoughts
like YOU do? Then maybe I could hypnotise
that idiot and make him forget about what
happened? Or else make him think I'm, like, the
REALLY SUPER SCARY kid, so he doesn't want to
rek with me?

What do you think? Can you help me out? I really

don't want to die at camp. Plz GBTM soon. Thanks a lot.

Good luck and have fun.

Harry Riddles

From Harry **to** Charley
Subject: The Dark Arts
8 February 20:10 GMT

Cuz –

I just wrote to Paul McKenna and I'm thinking if things work out with him, this could be a REALLY useful skill to have.

From Charley **to** Harry
Subject: Hypnotisers
9 February 13:35 MST

Yo –

You're going. Get used to it. Stop being a little worm!

————————————

From Harry **to** Charley
Subject: Worms
10 February 17:37 GMT

I'm not being a little worm. I just don't want to go to camp with Ed Bigstock. Plus, you know Kevin? He says he's bringing his guitar. If he does, I'm bringing my Xbox.

From Charley **to** Harry
10 February 12:51 MST

Forget it. U won't be allowed.

From Harry **to** Paul McKenna
Subject: The Dark Arts
10 February 21:04 GMT

Dear Paul McKenna,

My sister just told me you don't share your
hypnotiser skills with anybody, cos that stuff is top
secret and if I started doing what you do, I could
put you out of a job.

So here's another idea. How about you just
hypnotise ME instead? If you can make ME not
scared of the dark, OR Ed Bigstock, then that could
work out pretty good for me too. What do you
think? Good plan? Great! Can we do it tomorrow?
I don't have much time left, cos I'm getting put on
the bus really soon.

BTW, do you have Skype? That would probably be best, cos my mum doesn't like me giving out my phone number.

Good luck and have fun.

Harry Riddles

10 February 21:23 GMT

 Kid Zombie: Walnut? You online?

 Goofykinggrommet: Uh-huh.

 Kid Zombie: I'm so dead.

 Goofykinggrommet: What's the matter?

Kid Zombie: U know what Bigstock told me today in maths?

 Goofykinggrommet: What?

 Kid Zombie: He said when we're at camp, he's gonna put my hand in cold water when I'm asleep. Then I'm gonna wet the bed.

 Goofykinggrommet: What did u say?

 Kid Zombie: Nothing.

 Goofykinggrommet: From what I hear, your hand goes in the water, you wet the bed.

Kid Zombie: I know. Now I REALLY don't want to go to this camp.

From Harry **to** Andy McNab
Subject: Being brave
11 February 20:22 GMT

Dear Andy McNab, kick-ass soldier and author of
some really cool soldiering books, hi there!

My dad said if there's one guy out there who
knows how to deal with being scared, it's you. He's
read most of your books and he told me when I'm
a big kid, I should read 'em, cos I'd learn lots of
useful survival stuff (like
maybe how to give Ed
Bigstock the full beans
with a Vulcan Death
Hold).

But I don't have time to read your books before I
get sent away, so I thought I'd write to you and see

if maybe you could help me out, cos I don't know who else to ask.

I'm ten years old and, basically, I get really scared of the dark. If I have to sleep in a room without a light, I don't sleep. For one night, that would be OK (kind of), but I have to go to camp for four nights and five days, which is longer than I've been anywhere on my own before, so I know I'm also gonna get really HOMESICK.

I don't want to make an idiot of myself and have to get my mum to pick me up, so if you have any gr8 advice on how to be BRAVE, please write back. Thanks a lot for reading this.

Good luck and have fun.

Harry Riddles

Messages

KIDZOMBIE

 mickrock1: kid zombie you r a total fail!!!

 melonman: hahaha ragequitter!!!

 peanut2065: kid zombie u suck raw eggs!

 kidzombie: I didn't rage quit!!!

 darkassassin300: u quit cos u r like all newbs. Don't know how 2 play in team. U want a rematch? I'll rek u again!!!

12 February 17:08

 Kid Zombie: Walnut, u there?

 Goofykinggrommet: I'm here.

 Kid Zombie: I gotta rematch with darkassassin300!!!!!!!!!!

 Goofykinggrommet: When?

Kid Zombie: Next Tuesday at 8.

 Goofykinggrommet: Won't you be at camp?

 Kid Zombie: Oops.

Messages
KIDZOMBIE

 Kid Zombie: Can we change date, plz?

 darkassassin300: U trying 2 bail again?

 Kid Zombie: No! But I won't have an Xbox!!!!!!

 darkassassin300: u don't make it, u lose. End of.

World of ZOMBIES
COMMUNITY FORUM

12 February 17:20

 Goofykinggrommet: What did he say?

 Kid Zombie: If I don't play, I lose.

 Goofykinggrommet: What r u gonna do?

 Kid Zombie: I don't know.

Goofykinggrommet: Well, that sucks.

 Kid Zombie: It does if you want to get on the HandControllerz Team.

 Goofykinggrommet: What do you want to play now?

 Kid Zombie: How am I going to get my Xbox into this place?

 Goofykinggrommet: Not gonna happen, Harry. Do it next year.

 Kid Zombie: I don't want to do it NEXT year. I want to do it THIS year. Maybe I just got to get my parents to understand that I really, REALLY need to do this.

Goofykinggrommet: Yeah? How r u gonna do that?

From Harry **to** Mo Farah@mofarah.com
Subject: Sticking together
12 February 18:12 GMT

Dear Mo Farah, England's greatest living (or dead) athlete, hi there!

Imagine you had not been allowed to enter the London Olympics. Now imagine you were not even given the CHANCE to do your trial for the

Olympic team, cos your mum and dad sent you away to some stupid activity camp for half term. Well, that's what I've got to deal with, and it's not fair.

My name is Harry. I'm ten years old and basically I have a really important one v one death match next Tuesday. This match is like the Olympic trials for gamers like me, who play *World of Zombies*. If I can kick a TON of zombie rear, I will be selected to play for the brilliant HandControllerz Team in the first ever *World of Zombies* eSports Spectacular up at Wembley Arena (which, BTW, will be pretty UNBELIEVABLE). But I'm going to miss my trial unless somebody can help convince my mum and dad to let me stay home over half term and have my death match. That's why I'm writing to you. This sporting event is my big chance to make Cornwall proud. As one sportsman talking to

another, we need to STICK TOGETHER. Please help
me achieve my dream. Thanks a lot for reading
this.

Good luck and have fun.

Harry Riddles

From Harry **to** Jeremy Corbyn
Subject: Zombies & Schools
12 February 21:00 GMT

Dear Jeremy Corbyn, Leader of the Labour Party,
hi there!

As leader of the opposition, my dad says you're
going to need all the help you can get to make it
into Number 10. Well here's a great idea for you.
Let's make eSports compulsory in all schools!
Let's get kids gaming more! And let's make Britain
GREAT at *World of Zombies*!

As a sportsman, I'm finding it really tough to
become the elite player I want to be, when I don't
get the right support at home from my family,
or my school. I have a big *World of Zombies* trial
coming up, which I'm now probably going to have

to miss, because of my parents, Mr Forbes and this kid Kevin.

Can you write to my mum and dad and tell them that the Labour Party supports eSports for kids? Plus maybe a letter to Mr Forbes at my school?

If I was allowed to take my Xbox with me to activity camp, that would definitely help get this ball rolling in the right direction. Unfortunately, this ball isn't rolling anywhere UNLESS my parents get a nice letter from someone important like you. So what do you think? Can you help me out? Great!

BTW, when I wrote to David Cameron to offer him the chance to rent our house in the summer, he basically wrote back a really cool letter. So can you make it two for two? I would really appreciate it (and might even join your Labour Party when I'm bigger). Thanks a lot!

Good luck and have fun.

Harry Riddles

CHAPTER FIVE
WELCOME TO
WHIPPINGTON

From Mum **to** Harry
Subject: Growing up
15 February 14:20 GMT

Dear Harry,

Now that you are safely on your way to your first ever camp,
I just wanted to write and tell you how PROUD we are of you.
I hope you don't feel we pushed you into doing something
you didn't want to do, but I feel sure once you get to camp,
you'll have a GREAT time. So enjoy yourself and we'll see you on
Thursday!

Lots of love,

Mum xxx

From Harry **to** Mum
Subject: Growing up
15 February 15:04 GMT

Dear Mum,

Mr Forbes just came down the coach and told us who's sleeping in whose room. You know who's in my room? Bigstock and Kevin. So that sucks. Luckily Bulmer is too, otherwise I'd tell you to come and pick me up right now, cos four nights sleeping in a room with Ed Bigstock is probably going to be worse than four nights sleeping in a bedroom with Charlotte. (Actually – scratch that. Nothing is worse than four nights in a bedroom with Charlotte.)

Anyway, Bigstock told me to start thinking of some scary ghost stories, cos that's what he says we're going to be doing in our dorm when we go to bed.

Why? Did Charlotte tell him something about me? She told me she would. And he keeps looking over at me and grinning, like he knows something I don't want him to know.

Harry

_____

From Mum **to** Harry
Subject: Growing Up
15 February 15:12 GMT

Dear Harry,

Of course Charlotte didn't tell him anything. She's your sister!

I know, but she hates me.
Harry

Your sister doesn't hate you.
Mum.

She does. She's always telling me she
hates me and I'm stupid, but I get it. She's a
psycho.

Your sister is not a psycho.

Whatever.

Just tell Ed you want to hear some funny stories, not ghost stories

Yeah, but Ed's not funny.

Then ignore him.

From Harry **to** Mum
Subject: Home
15 February 19:03 GMT

Dear Mum,

I tried ignoring him, but that didn't work. Then I tried calling you, but you guys are out. So here's my news: this place SUCKS!!! COME AND GET ME!!!

Harry

From Harry **to** Charley
Subject: Help
15 February 20:14 GMT

Dear Cuz –

Well, we're here, but I'll bet your camp was nothing like this dump. It really BLOWS. We got here late because our bus broke down and we had to change a tyre, so when we arrived it was raining and dark and there were no lights on and I'm like, "Great! Nobody's here! Let's go home!" But then this tall dude comes out with a torch. He says, "Hi! I'm Little Dave! Welcome to Whippington! We thought you guys would *never* get here!"

Before I can get a word out, Bigstock comes barging past me and says, "And miss going surfing?! And kayaking?! And abseiling?! And archery?!! And quad-biking?!?!! Are you *CRAZY*!!! Of course, we were going to make it!!! This is going to be the best holiday *EVER* – right, Harry?"

Sometimes I wish that kid would keep his big mouth shut (actually MOST times). Only an idiot would think this place is gonna be GOOD TIMES. But I don't say that, cos Little Dave goes, "Well, if it's fun you kids are after, you've come to the *right* place! Come on in!"

So we go inside this old house and it's really dark, and really cold, and me and Bulmer are looking at each other thinking this is a HUGE mistake. And it all gets, like, ten times worse when Bigstock comes up behind me and goes, "BOO!" I jump. He laughs. Then Georgia Gardener goes, "So what if Harry is scared of the dark? A lot of kids get scared of the dark! Right, Harry?"

I go, "Who says I'm scared of the dark?"

And Bigstock goes, "Your *sister*!"

So Charlotte dobbed me in. When I see her, I'm gonna hack her Facebook account and then I'm gonna post on her home page those stupid photos of her wearing braces on her teeth. And if anybody asks me, I'll tell 'em my sister *does* have a big butt.

BTW, I'm already sick of Kevin and his stupid guitar. Him and Jess have been singing all the way here. If he starts singing in the dorm

tonight, I'm definitely going to sleep in the
bathroom!

Harry

From Harry **to** Paul McKenna
Subject: The Dark Arts
15 February 20:22 GMT

Dear Paul McKenna,

I don't know if you saw my last email, but things are going downhill fast. I'm only hours away from bedtime, and Bigstock is on to me big time. We need to talk. Plz mail me. But be quick, OK? This is REALLY important! Thanks a lot!

Harry

From Charley **to** Harry
Subject: Help
15 February 13:25 MST

Squid –

If Ed Bigstock thinks he's gonna scare you, scare him back!

From Harry **to** Charley
15 February 20:40 GMT

How? The kid has NO FEAR. But, you'll never guess what just happened... My phone pings while we're eating dinner. So Bigstock goes, "Is that your little mummy, Harry? Maybe she'll come and get you! Ha ha!" And I'm like, GREAT!

But you know who it was?

_____

From Charley **to** Harry
15 February 13:42 MST

Who?

From Harry **to** Charley
15 February 20:43 GMT

Andy McNab.

Andy McNab wrote back
to you?
Charley.

Yeah.
Harry

Bull.

I told you writing's a good
thing to do.

What did McNab say?

From Harry **to** Charley
Subject: McNab
15 February 20:54 GMT

Basically, this:

@The_Real_McNab

Harry,

I think you're probably already braver than anyone else you know, because deep down everyone is scared of something. It could be the dark. Or feeling homesick. Or something else. But what makes you brave is that you want to try and overcome your fear, when maybe your mates would just cover it up. And covering up can make things a lot worse.

So I don't think you'll have problems when you go on your school trip. In fact, I think you'll be able to help your friends, who probably will feel just like you do, because you're already a brave kid.

Andy McNab

Messages **Charley to Harry** Clear

He really wrote that?
Charley.

Yeah.
Harry

You didn't make it up?

No. He wrote it.

That is like *so* cool.

I know.

94

So what are you gonna do?

I'm going to tell my mum that my sister definitely dobbed me in.

Yeah, but r u gonna stay?

I dunno. Mum hasn't got back to me, so I can't go anywhere even if I wanted to. Plus, I told Bulmer that if he's not getting picked up, then I'll stay with him. He said he just wants to go home and be with his dog and not Ed Bigstock. I told him he can borrow a bear if it makes him feel better, cos my mum packed three for me. I think he's gonna borrow one. And if this place still sucks in the morning, we've got the whole day to get rescued.

Once you guys have done a night, it'll get a lot easier. I promise

Not with Bigstock. He just told us him and Kevin have got a little surprise waiting for us.

What did you say?

I said, Don't bother trying anything with a bucket of water, cos I'm keeping my hands under the covers.

From Harry **to** Andy McNab
Subject: Fear
16 February 07:45 GMT

Dear Andy McNab,

Last night before bed I showed Bulmer what
you wrote and he said you're right. We need
to FACE OUR FEARS. So we told Bigstock we
don't need the light on to sleep, cos we're good
without it. So Bigstock turns it off. Then he shuts
the door. And we're just about to climb into
our beds, when the door of the closet suddenly
swings wide open and Kevin jumps out going,
"AAAAAAAAAAAAAAAAA!!!"

Well, that did it. We freaked. Luckily, when Bulmer
freaks, he breaks wind. A LOT. And when Bulmer
breaks wind, you have to leave the room, OR

keep that door wide open, cos the room will smell worse than one of Farmer Harold's fields after he's been out with the muck spreader. So Bigstock starts holding his nose going, "Oh my God, Bulmer – you are so *disgusting!*"

Which was great, cos Bigstock had to keep the door OPEN for the rest of the night. So we faced our fears and it worked (kind of). I'm just keeping my fingers crossed we have curry tonight. Otherwise we might be in big trouble if Bulmer runs out of gas.

Thanks a lot for the really great advice.

Good luck and have fun.

Harry

From Harry **to** Charley
Subject: Bigstock
16 February 08:50 GMT

Cuz –

At breakfast this morning Little Dave asked us
if anybody in our group liked to make films and
wanted to keep a record of our time at camp.
So Bigstock points his finger at me and tells him
I'm a filmmaker – which I thought was him being
half decent for once, cos I guessed he was talking
about my 'Eat the Parents' zombie film. But when
Little Dave says, "What kind of films do you make,
Harry?" Bigstock starts laughing and tells him I
make these stupid videos of me playing *World of
Zombies*. Which is true. I do make videos of my
battles and sometimes I post 'em up on the *WoZ*
website, but those are just gaming videos. They

aren't gonna win me any Oscars.

Well, it turns out Little Dave is a mad, crazy GAMER just like me. So me and him start talking about Carpocalypse Now and he tells me how much he *loves* the game, how really *great* it is, but how he can never get past Level 1.

So now I'm thinking, OMG – this is, like, so cool! This old guy likes *WoZ*! Maybe this camp isn't the dump I thought it was after all. So then Jessica starts telling Little Dave that if he likes to play *WoZ*, then I'm the right kid to talk to, cos I play *WoZ* a LOT. So he asks me if I'm good and Jessica says, "Good? Harry's almost MLG – right, Harry?"

I go, "Well, I could be if I could do my trial!" And Little Dave goes, "What trial, Harry?" So I tell him about my one v one death match with darkassassin300 on Tuesday night, and he's like, "You have a one v one death match?"

I'm like, "Yeah!" And then I realise if Little Dave plays *WoZ*, then he must have an XBOX!!! And if he's got an Xbox then, OMG I could play my death match!!! So I'm about to ask him if we can do a trade, when Bigstock jumps in and shouts, "You can't let Harry play *video* games at ACTIVITY CAMP!!!"

I say, "Why not?"

And he says, "Cos it's AGAINST CAMP RULES!!!" Then he says he's going off to find Mr Forbes and see what *he* has to say. The thing with Bigstock is, his parents won't buy him an Xbox, or a PlayStation, so he HATES video games and everybody (like me) who plays them, cos he's not allowed (plus when he is, he sucks anyway).

So then Little Dave asks about the film – can I make it for him? I tell him if nobody else is volunteering, I'll do it. Which was cool. But then Little Dave divides us up into teams. Did you do this at your camp? Have a competition to see which team can score the *most* points over the three days, and the winner gets a little cup?

Well, we're doing it, and I didn't think it was a big deal, until Bigstock bet Jessica that his team will SLAUGHTER our team, and the losers will have to do a *dare*. And as soon as I heard that I thought we could be in LOTS of trouble, because basically Bigstock's a lunatic, and if it's him choosing a dare for us to do, we might die.

The only good thing is, he LOVES being on camera, cos he thinks he could be an action movie star like Daniel Craig. Plus, he's just started his own Instagram account, so he needs to put cool stuff up on it. So I figure if I can get that idiot to think more about how he looks for the camera than on winning his team activities, we might get out of here in one piece.

Harry to Dad

Pups – first challenge is quad-biking. Three laps round a course marked out in a field. Good news is, I have to make a really cool film, which might just save our bacon.
Harry

If u r making a film, don't forget to write up a film log like I showed you.
Dad.

<u>Harry's Film Log:</u>

Day One:

Scene 1: Exterior. Quad-biking. Day

Race 1

Me versus Kevin and some other kids, filmed by Bulmer. Unfortunately, Kevin wins easily. Fortunately, Bulmer is more interested in filming Georgia and Jessica than me. Kevin gets angry with Bulmer, cos there is no footage of him winning the race, only stuff of Georgia and Jessica making funny faces and fooling around. I think Bulmer might like Georgia more than a little.

Race 2

Jessica was beating all the girls until
Georgia fell off. Then Jessica stopped to
help her, so we didn't win. But we beat
Bigstock's team, so that's one point each.

Race 3

The decider. Bulmer is not sure he can
deliver the goods against ace quad-
biker Ed Bigstock, who does not stop
bragging to anybody who will listen
about his in-credible quad-biking skills.
I take Bigstock to one side and ask him
for an interview for my film, which he
is excited to give. Once he has fixed his
hair for, like, the millionth time, I ask him

how many followers he has on his new Instagram account. He says he has about eight, but two of them are his parents. I tell him if he can do a crazy rooster tail, or a big wheelie when he comes past me on the quad, then I can film it and we can post it up on his Instagram account and he'll definitely get into double digits with new followers. Bigstock likes this idea A LOT. He even thanks me for it. Ha!

When Bigstock goes off to get his quad, Jessica says she doesn't think he'll be stupid enough to show off and fall off. I tell her nobody should underestimate Ed Bigstock. When it comes to him doing stupid stuff, all the bets are off.

Lap 1

Biggy pulls out a big lead and Bulmer stalls on the hill. When Bigstock comes past the finish line, I stand in the track and yell for a wheelie, but he plays it safe and I get a lens full of mud.

Lap 2

Biggy now miles ahead of the field.

Bulmer last. As Bigstock comes out of the turn on to the straight, I yell, "ROOSTER TAIL AND WHEELIE, ED!!! COME ON!!!"

But again, Bigstock ignores me.

Lap 3

Last lap and last chance. Bulmer stalls his quad on the finishing straight and Bigstock roars past him. With the victory flag in his sight, I jump out on the track and yell, "Thumbs up for the camera, Ed???" And finally, Bigstock takes the bait. He turns to give me and the camera a victorious two-thumbs up. But he doesn't notice the kid in front of him

has stopped to wipe his goggles. Bigstock
rams the back marker and falls off. Some
other kid wins and Bigstock accuses
me of sabotaging his race. I tell him he
should not think of it as a defeat, but
as a victory for increasing his follower-
count on Instagram, cos his crash was
SPECTACULAR. He's not sure this is a

good trade-off, but who cares - it's 1—1
after the first activity. A GREAT RESULT
for us!

Yay!!!

Harry to Charley

2-1 up at end of Day 1!!!
Harry

Go, Smurf! What activity?
Charley.

Surfing!

U won?

Uh-huh.

How?

Bigstock.

What did he do now?

He almost ended up in
Cuba!!!

What r u talking about,
Harry?

From Harry **to** Charley
Subject: Bigstock
16 February 18:03 GMT

OK, so basically we get to lunch after the quad challenge and it's a wind-up session with Bigstock, cos Kevin's told him I'd tricked him. So he turns up at lunch and he starts telling me and Bulmer we'd better be ready for some super-scary stories after LIGHTS-OUT tonight cos Bulmer's gas trick will NOT work two nights on the trot! So we go, "Why's that, Ed?" And he bangs

down this can
of air freshener
that he's
just stolen
from the
bathroom.

I tell him we don't care about the air freshener. And we don't care if the door's shut, cos we're facing our fears, just like McNab said. But he laughs and says we'll see how long that lasts when we hear his horror story, cos it's SICK!!! Then he and Kevin walk away high-fiving.

Anyway, after lunch we climb into the minibus to head down to the beach for surfing lessons and Bigstock slides into the seat in front of me and Bulmer, cos he wants to creep us out with his stupid horror story. I tell him we don't want to hear his story, we want to watch this hilarious video of a kid crashing his quad bike into the other kid when he loses the race. He asks me to show him the video and only then does he realise the video is of HIM – which made him really mad.

So then he grabs the phone off me and starts

telling us his story and I try not to listen, but it's hard when his face is about six inches from mine. Anyway, this story is about a family that's like MY family, cos the dad's a WRITER and he's married with two kids, just like me and Charlotte.

So this writer guy moves his family down from the city to live in an old farmhouse in some place like Cornwall and everything is great for the family – the kids start a new school, Dad starts writing a new book, Mum starts making her art. But then one day the boy goes up into the attic to explore. And he finds this box full of old Super 8 films. So he starts looking at these old films on a projector. And these films are home movies about the LAST family that lived in the house – which the boy thinks is pretty cool. Until he gets to the bit where the kids get MURDERED!!!

Well, by now we're close to the beach and me and Bulmer are thinking this is a really scary story. What are we going to do if the door's shut, the light's out, and Bigstock starts telling us the rest of THAT one tonight? Maybe we'll have to go sleep in the bathroom after all.

Luckily, we get down on to the coast road and Bigstock gets distracted, cos he sees the sea and it's, like, ENORMOUS. There are white horses from one side of the bay right across to the other. So Ed stops telling his horror story and switches back to doing what he likes doing best: showing off. He goes over to Georgia Gardener and starts bragging to her about the last time him and his dad went surfing down at Milook in Cornwall and none of the local guys were out catching waves, cos the waves were so BIG.

From Charley **to** Harry
Subject: Bigstock
16 February 11:04 MST

Sounds like Bigstock BS.

From Harry **to** Charley
16 February 18:08 GMT

That's what me and Jessica thought. But Georgia
Gardener was sucking up to him, cos I think she
thinks he's really cool. So she's like, "Oh, I can't
wait to see you surf, Ed! I bet you're gonna be just
AMAZING!!!" (Barf).

From Charley **to** Harry
16 February 11:12 MST

So then?

From Harry **to** Charley
16 February 18:23 GMT

So then we get down to the beach and Georgia goes, "Will you be surfing those big waves, Ed?" And Bigstock's like, "Those monsters? Of course I will, Georgia!" So me and Bulmer are like: well, if you can ride them, you DESERVE to win this challenge, cos they are like HUGE!

But once we've got into our wetsuits and have gone through all the paddling and how-to-stand-up-on-your-board training drills down on the beach, Little Dave and the other instructor, Surfer Pete, tell us that they don't want *anybody* getting out of their depth, because there's a strong rip that could take us all the way over to Cuba! So Ed was *not* allowed to paddle out and catch the big waves, which was good news for us, cos we'd have a better chance of winning the challenge. But not so good for him, cos he couldn't show off.

Anyway, we get into the water and we start catching these little white-water waves, which, BTW, was lots of fun. Even Bulmer stood up (for about two seconds), which got him pretty pumped. But Bigstock was getting bored, cos this was beginners' stuff. So he catches a wave in, gets out the water and starts walking up the beach with his board to some rocks that stick out into the sea. We're watching and thinking: what's he doing now? But we don't say anything, because if he isn't in the water with us, we don't have to listen to him telling us we all suck.

Ten minutes later there's a major panic when Little Dave sees Bigstock paddling out from the rocks down the beach. Little Dave starts yelling at

Bigstock, but the wind is blowing so hard I don't think he hears.

So we all get told to get out of the water, and I go and fetch the camera, but when I get back everybody is now really worried, cos Bigstock is like this tiny black speck way, WAY out in the distance, and Little Dave and Surfer Pete are still maybe 150 metres from getting to him on their surfboards.

So we're watching from the beach when we see this BIG WAVE come. And we're thinking OMG this wave will CRUSH Bigstock. But he starts paddling for it. And the wave picks him up. And he catches the wave and jumps to his feet. And all the girls start cheering, cos this wave is BIGGER than him. But then he gets to the bottom, starts his turn and WIPES OUT. When his head pops up in all this bubbling white water, the girls are now going, "Is he going to be all right out there?" Cos another wave breaks on top of him. Then ANOTHER. And when he finally pops up again, we can see he's now starting to panic, which is pretty scary to watch.

Luckily Little Dave and Surfer Pete got to him before he went under again. But it was twenty-five minutes before they got him back to shore. And when they dragged him up on to the beach, for once Bigstock was lost for words.

<u>Harry's Film Log:</u>

Scene 2: Exterior. Surfing. Day

*No footage of surfing — until Bigstock
gets in trouble. I film the rescue by Little
Dave and Surfer Pete. Jessica gets Bigstock
a towel and tells him we were all really
worried for him. Most of the other kids
ignore him, because they had to stop surfing
when he needed rescuing so they're, like,
really annoyed. I ask him for a few words for
the camera but he doesn't want to talk to
me. Instead he pokes his tongue out.*

*Little Dave awards the surf challenge to all
the teams equally — except Bigstock's, cos
he said being in the water is about staying
SAFE in the water, not doing what Ed did,*

which was really not cool.

Scene 3: Interior. The bus ride back to camp.
Day

Bigstock is in a bad mood on the bus. So he
comes over to us to continue his horror story,
cos I think he thinks it will make him feel
better. But he doesn't get far, cos Bulmer
starts breaking wind again. Bigstock has to
move seats.

Scene 4: Interior/Exterior. Loading the boards
back in the board shed. Day

Bigstock suddenly drops his board and runs
out. Won't tell us why.

How's camp?

Walnut

OK.

Harry

Can u play ur death match?

I'm working on it.

From Harry **to** Ant & Dec
Subject: Scary stuff
16 February 20:11 GMT

Dear Ant & Dec, my mum's favourite TV presenters, hi there!

As the guys who host *I'm a Celebrity, Get Me Out Of Here*, you've seen your fair share of numpties over the years. But let's say you had one idiot, who has absolutely NO fear of ANYTHING – what dare would you make him do?

Me and Bulmer have thought about all the stuff most people get frightened of – ghosts, bogeymen, the dark, snakes, blood, clowns, dead people alive in movies, climbing up church steeples, but we don't think ANY of that will work with this moron, cos he thinks all that stuff is for babies. What would you make him do for one of your Bushtucker Trials?

Plz GBTM soon.

Good luck and have fun.

Harry Riddles

Harry's Film Log

Scene 5: Interior. Tea time. Night

Bulmer has the cooks in the kitchen and Georgia Gardener lol-ing with his funny impersonation of a famous cook who swears a lot. Bigstock gets jealous and tries to steal Bulmer's cake (as usual), but Ed drops the cake plate and screams when a small spider lands on his shoulder. We now know Bigstock HATES spiders. This could be just the weapon we need!

From Harry **to** Sir David Attenborough
Subject: Spiders
16 February 20:53 GMT

Dear Sir David Attenborough, wildlife expert and maker of some really, really cool TV shows about animals, hi there!

My biology teacher, Mrs Rawlins, said that you once said, 'Humans are a plague on the earth and need to be controlled by limiting population growth!' I agree. Let's start with Ed Bigstock. This kid's almost eleven and he's Mount Joseph's very own Natural Ecological Disaster. I mean it. If Ed comes into a classroom looking for somebody to wrestle, that classroom will empty faster than you can say 'Tsunami!'

Me and Bulmer are sharing a dorm with this

idiot for, like, the next three nights and we had
no idea how we were going to survive – until this
afternoon when we discovered he HATES spiders.

If we can find some, we might be able to get some sleep tonight. Our problem is, we can't. We've looked in the board shed, Bulmer's checked the toilets, I've looked under floorboards, but no luck. Where else can we look?

Plz GBTM soon.

Good luck and have fun.

Harry Riddles

From Harry **to** Charley
Subject: Buddy & Boris
17 February 07:04 GMT

Dear Cuz –

You know I told you about our spider problem
here at camp? Well, we couldn't find any,
but we did find something just as good –
COCKROACHES!!!

We figured that if we picked out two of the
biggest, ugliest roaches and took them up to
the dorm, we could cause some MAYHEM when
Bigstock insisted on keeping that door shut and
the light off to scare us with his creepy horror
story.

So we find two roaches, name them Buddy and

Boris and put them in matchboxes to take to the dorm, while Bigstock was still fixing his hair for bed (the kid spends more time on his hair than my sister).

Anyway, just before I get over to my bed, Buddy escapes from my matchbox, drops on to Bigstock's pillow, and disappears between the sheets. So Buddy is now somewhere in Bigstock's BED!!! And before I can dig him out, Bigstock comes bouncing into the dorm, and he's now back to his old, nasty self again, after a couple of quiet hours when he was sulking after surfing. So he pulls back the sheet, jumps into his bed, and asks us to remind him *where* exactly we had got to in the horror story? Was it the bit where the kids get hung from a tree in the back yard? Or the bit where another kid is found at the bottom of a swimming pool, tied to a chair?

Well, neither me nor Bulmer feel any great desire to tell Bigstock about the cockroach situation at the bottom of his bed, so we just sit and wait. Then, just as he starts telling us about how the dad discovers that the murders are the work of a SERIAL KILLER, he suddenly goes, "Ow!" and leaps out of bed, saying something just BIT him.

Well me and Bulmer are now trying really hard
not to laugh, cos we don't want to give the game
away. And that's when Mr Forbes comes into the
room asking Bigstock what he's doing out of bed?
Ed tells him he just got bitten by something.

So now I get out my phone and I start filming, cos
this is funny stuff. Bulmer is enjoying himself too.
He starts having payback on Ed for all his chubby
jokes. So he's like, "Was that bite like a *spider's*
bite maybe, Ed? What does a spider's bite *feel*
like? Do you think it's still in your bed?"

Bigstock tells Bulmer to shut up, but he's gone
completely white – just like one of his ghosts. Mr
Forbes strips the bed, but they can't find Buddy.
So they make the bed again and Mr Forbes leaves
the dorm, but Ed now looks so pale and shaky
that I take pity on him and decide to tell him that I

think it was only a cockroach.

Well that did it. Bigstock jumps out of bed, yells for Mr Forbes, and when Mr Forbes comes back in the room, Bigstock tells him I put a roach in his bed.

I had to do a LOT of explaining after that, but in the end Mr Forbes believed I didn't put Buddy in Bigstock's bed ON PURPOSE and tells Bigstock that if he doesn't want any more incidents with cockroaches, he should stop trying to freak us out and just leave the door open, and not tell spooky stories. Which is what happened.

My problem now is, Bigstock has just come down for breakfast and he's complaining of earache. Do cockroaches crawl inside ears? I'm hoping Buddy hasn't crawled into Bigstock's ear, cos he's

not going to like it down there. Even if he is a
cockroach. Do you think I should tell him? If Buddy
is in his ear, Bigstock WILL kill me.

Harry

<u>Harry's Film Log</u>

Scene 6: Bedtime with Bigstock and Buddy.

Bigstock meets Buddy and loses his cool.
After Forbes leaves for the final time, Kevin
starts singing, "Some think cockroaches are
a pest! But that's the insect I love best!"
Bigstock tells him to shut it. That Kevin
certainly knows a lot of songs.

CHAPTER TEN
A HUNTING ACCIDENT

How was last night?
Dad

Good.
Harry

No problems with Ed?

No. Buddy and Boris kept him quiet.

Who?

Doesn't matter.

So what are you doing today?

Well, we just did archery.

Great! How did that go?

Good. No one got killed.

What's *that* mean?

From Harry **to** Dad
Subject: Ed
17 February 11:58 GMT

OK, so basically after breakfast we go down to the field archery place and Ed starts telling Kevin and Georgia how him and his dad are, like, these expert bowmen, so this challenge should be POINTS ON THE BOARD for their team.

When I hear that I think, OK. Maybe I don't need to film this. But Bigstock calls me over. He tells me I should forget about shooting a bow, because I will probably suck. Instead, I should film him, because he will be totally BRILLIANT.

So I tell him I don't feel like filming him, or anybody else, cos I want to try shooting a bow, cos it looks good fun. Well, he didn't like that. But I say I don't care. I want to try archery and be like that guy in *Assassin's Creed*. Or the girl in *Hunger Games* who shoots down spaceships!

Well, he starts laughing and telling me I'm such a loser, cos that stuff is *not real*. Real is what him and his dad do when they go off duck hunting in Louisiana. And then he starts telling Georgia about his last hunting trip, when him and his dad were down in some swamp, and the ducks were out on the water. And they were sneaking through the reeds. And just as he gets to the bit where he pulls back his bowstring to show us how he took his shot – *ping!* He snaps the bowstring!

OMG, funny! But I didn't get it on film! So now I'm thinking maybe there might be some good stuff coming my way if I start filming him and I won't need to trick him into doing something stupid, cos we're talking about Ed Bigstock here. He's already stupid.

So I get my phone out and the instructor comes over and gives Bigstock another bow and asks him to show his pull, cos he thinks his pull could be the reason the string snapped. But just as Bigstock takes the bow and tells the instructor he doesn't need any instruction, Bulmer shouts, "Pheasants!"

So we all look up as these two pheasants come flying right over our heads. And that's when we hear a loud *thwang!* And Bigstock's arrow is shooting straight up towards the birds!

Well, the instructor sees the arrow and yells, "RUN!" because what goes up, must come down. So we all scatter.

Luckily, nobody got hurt. But the instructor grabs Bigstock's bow and he's like, "I didn't do it on purpose! It was a hunting accident! The string slipped!"

Anyway, Bigstock got banned from archery, but they still beat us, because Kevin found out he's like Robin Hood with a bow and never misses. But archery was really cool, and maybe I should save up and buy a bow. Then you and me could practise out in the shed?

From Dad **to** Harry
Subject: Ed
17 February 12:08 GMT

We can do that.

From Harry **to** Dad
17 February 12:09 GMT

Cool! The only bad news is him and Kevin have now told me and Bulmer they know *exactly* what dare we will be doing when we lose the challenge.

Three guesses what that's going to be.

What?
Dad

Locking us in the woodshed.
Harry.

U don't have to do that!

Those are the rules, pups.

If Ed's bullying you, go talk
to Mr Forbes.

It's OK. I'm fine.

I'll call Forbes!

DON'T! As McNab said, I'm facing my fears. So plz stay out of it.

From Harry **to** Charley
Subject: White Water Kayaking.
17 February 17:04 GMT

Cuz —

Here's what our kayak teacher told us before we got on the river this afternoon.

1. Check the drain bung of your kayak.

2. Make sure your dry suit is zipped up, or you'll get wet.

3. Don't forget where we stop because if you see the bridge, you've gone too far...

Easy, right? Can't get any of that wrong? Well,

Bigstock did. He genuinely was *great* at kayaking, and as we went down the river he kept doing these Eskimo rolls to show Georgia how brilliant he was. Bulmer wasn't impressed. Neither was Kevin. I didn't take the camera (which made Bigstock mad) cos I didn't want it to get wet, so most of what happened on the water I missed.

But I think the water was so cold, it must have frozen Bigstock's brain, cos when we were supposed to get off the river and pull the kayaks into this sandy beach area, Bigstock kept paddling.

So we yell at him, but he doesn't hear. Or maybe he does, but he's not stopping. Either way, he disappears down this weir ahead and we have to spend the next 45 minutes following him downriver in the minibus, until we can pick him up from the next town on the river. When he finally gets out the water, I get out my camera and Bulmer goes over and asks him if he's had his hearing checked recently, cos he seems to have missed the briefing.

Well, that was a mistake, cos Bigstock rips into Bulmer about his weight, which made everybody embarrassed for Bulmer.

We're now even in the challenges, but what do we dare him if we beat him?

Harry

From Charley **to** Harry
Subject: The Master of Horror
17 February 10:12 MST

Smurf,

You wanna know how to scare Bigstock? Ask Stephen King. He's the Master of All Horror. He'll know.

From Harry **to** Stephen King
Subject: Horror
17 February 17:52 GMT

Dear Stephen King, Master of All Horror, hi there!

We have to come up with a dare for this kid who loves all the scary stuff. My friend Bulmer wants to put his head in the toilet and keep it there while we flush it, but that's probably cos he's sick of Bigstock calling him 'the chubster'. My other friend Jessica says she wants to dare him to ask Georgia Gardener out, cos Georgia likes him, but I don't want that to happen, cos I know Bulmer likes her too (and she'd be better off going out with him, cos he's a much nicer kid. Plus, he's much funnier). I know Bigstock *hates* spiders, so we could dare him to put his hand in a box full of them, but we have to find them first, and there aren't many around here. So I'm looking for some new ideas.

What scares you?

Plz GBTM soon.

Good luck and have fun.

Harry Riddles

Bulmer to Harry

Where u?
Bulmer

Be there soon!
Harry

Zoo game starts in 5
minutes!!!

Start without me.

Why aren't you here? U said
u would be! We need u!!!
Jessica

Got something I have to do.
Sorry!!!
Harry

But where r u?

17 February 19:53

 Kid Zombie: Walnut - you online?

 Goofykinggrommet: Hey Harry! R u still at camp?

 Kid Zombie: Yeah.

 Goofykinggrommet: Cool! Whose Xbox are you using?

Kid Zombie: Little Dave's.

 Goofykinggrommet: Who?

 Kid Zombie: He's one of the guys who works here.

 Goofykinggrommet: Are u allowed?

 Kid Zombie: Haven't asked.

 Goofykinggrommet: R u gonna get in trouble??

Kid Zombie: I won't be on long. But I got my one v one death match in like 5 minutes and I don't want to miss it!

 Goofykinggrommet: What if someone sees you?

 Kid Zombie: OMG Forbes outside the window!!! Gotta go.

From Harry **to** Charley
Subject: Mistake
17 February 21:05 GMT

Cuz –

I think I just made a BIG mistake.

From Charley **to** Harry
Subject: Mistake
17 February 14:08 MST

What happened, Squid?

From Harry **to** Charley
17 February 21:10 GMT

OK, so all day I've been thinking, do I or do I not sneak into the staffroom where Little Dave keeps his Xbox to play my death match? If I ask him, he's not going to let me, cos if he lets me, then every kid here will want to use it. And I can't tell anybody, or ask anybody what they think, cos nobody will tell me it's a good idea.

So by the end of the day, I'm thinking probably the best thing for me to do is NOT do it. But on the ride back in the minibus from kayaking, Bigstock made fun of me in front of Jessica by telling her I'm basically athletically handicapped and an embarrassment at all activities. I was pretty average at archery. I was the slowest on the river in a kayak. Even Kevin beat me on a quad bike!

The only thing I'm good for is stupid video games!

Well, when everybody laughed at me I thought, you know what? You're right. Maybe that is all I'm good at. Maybe I should just try and be MLG and forget these stupid activities. So I decide to play my death match and let them go play the zoo game without me.

So I sneak off, but Mr Forbes comes looking for me and though I don't get caught, I don't get to stay on long enough to play my death match as Mr Forbes finds me and makes me go back and join the others. But when I get there the game is over and we've lost and Bigstock has made a fool out of Bulmer in front of Georgia again. So Bulmer is now really upset and is saying he's not coming to the disco tomorrow night, cos he's too embarrassed. And Jessica says this is all my fault.

From Charley **to** Harry
17 February 14:18 MST

How's this yr fault?

_____

From Harry **to** Charley
17 February 21:19 GMT

She says I put gaming before friends and if I'd
been there we might not have lost and Bigstock
wouldn't have picked on Bulmer, cos I would have
been filming him and making jokes. I said, "But I
really suck at activities and I just want to be good
at something." She said she _thought_ I was good at
being a friend, but now she's not so sure.

From Charley **to** Harry
17 February 14:22 MST

Cuz –

Don't worry about it. It will all blow over, but
you need to say sorry and make it up to them
(and maybe next time FORGET your death
match).

From Harry **to** Charley
17 February 21:23 GMT

I know.

From Mum **to** Harry
Subject: How's it going?
17 February 21:24 GMT

Dear Harry,

Can't wait to see you. Your dad and I will pick you up on
Thursday. How's it all going?
Mum xxx

From Harry **to** Mum
Subject: How's it going?
17 February 21:26 GMT

Well, it was going OK, but I just
did something stupid (kind of),
so now I'm trying to fix things
with my friends before I go to

bed. But I'll write more soon. Gotta go.

Love u Mum.

Bye!

Harry xxx

From Harry **to** Chris Brown
Subject: Busting moves
17 February 21:38 GMT

Dear Chris Brown, R & B superstar, hi there –

My friend Jessica said you and Usher are WAY
better dancers than Justin Timberlake or the King
of Pop, Michael Jackson. Well, tomorrow night I'm
going to have to bring something
to the dance floor if I want
to make things right with
Jessica. But I don't know
how to dance. Bulmer
says it's easy. But I don't
think he knows what he's
talking about. That's why
I'm writing to you. How do
I learn to do something really

cool before tomorrow night? Is that possible?

Plz GBTM soon,

Good luck and have fun.

Harry Riddles

From Harry **to** Calvin Harris
Subject: Floor fillers
17 February 21:43 GMT

Dear Calvin Harris, superstar DJ, hi there!

I'm in the doghouse with my friends and I need A LOT of help to get out. Tomorrow night we have our end of camp disco, which basically means we all have to choose some cool songs to give to Little Dave and Mr Forbes, so they can get them downloaded and ready for us, but I don't know any pop songs. I talked to Jessica and Bulmer and also this kid Kevin, and asked them to give me a playlist so I could send it to you, cos I figured if you're the highest-paid DJ in the world, you're probably THE right guy who will know what's good and what's pants.

So here's my friend Bulmer's list. It's old skool, but that's what he listens to with his grandparents (where he basically lives): BTW – if you don't know these tunes, that's OK, cos I don't either.

Bulmer's List:

1) La Bamba – Richie Valens
2) Wipe Out – The Ventures
3) Build Me Up, Buttercup – Foundation
4) I'm a Believer – The Monkees
5) Like a Virgin – Madonna
6) Breakdance – Grandmaster Flash & The Furious Five

Kevin hates pop music, cos he's more an indie guy. So his list goes like this:

Kevin's List:

1) Heaven Knows I'm Miserable Now – The Smiths
2) Girlfriend in a Coma – The Smiths

He couldn't be bothered to think of any more, cos he thinks discos suck.

But Jessica LOVES pop music, so her list is like this:

Jessica's List:

1) Happy – Pharrell Williams
2) What Makes You Beautiful – One Direction
3) Call Me Maybe – Carly Rae Jepsen
4) Firework – Katy Perry
5) Beauty and a Beat – Justin Bieber and Nicky Minaj

When I talked to Little Dave he said him and the guys have their own tunes they play, like YMCA, Macarena, Cha Cha Slide and Superman.

Personally – I don't like any of that stuff, I prefer hip-hop. However, since you're a superstar DJ, what about you tell me some of *your* favourite tunes, then I can choose them and tell Jessica I've got some killer tunes for our disco and then maybe she won't be so mad at me. Can you do that for me? Great! Thanks a lot!

Good luck and have fun.

Harry Riddles

CHAPTER TWELVE
BUGHOLE

Harry

Me 2.
Jessica

Make it up to u tomorrow. Promise.

Make it up to Bulmer. He's your friend. U weren't there for him.

Yeah, but Bulmer

I don't want to speak to u either.

From Harry **to** Charley
Subject: Gaming
17 February 21:46 GMT

Cuz –

Maybe it's time 4 me to go home.

From Charley **to** Harry
Subject: Gaming
17 February 14:47 MST

Don't leave just cos you messed up. Sort the problem out, Smurf.

From Harry **to** Charley
17 February 21:48 GMT

I'm not leaving *just* cos I messed up (well maybe).

From Charley **to** Harry
17 February 14:49 MST

Sort it out.

From Harry **to** Charley
17 February 21:50 GMT

OK. Good idea (maybe).

OK. I'm trying to sort the problem out. But Bigstock is telling me his horror story and I'm getting really SCARED.
Harry

U know that serial killer? He's not really a serial killer!!!

He's called Bughole!!!

He KILLS families 4 FUN!!!

Then he takes a kid hostage!!!
ARRRGGHH!!!!

Back to his DEMON WORLD!!!

AND THEN STEALS THEIR SOUL!!!!!

Can't take any more!
Gonna sleep in the 🛁
Bye!

From Harry **to** Charley
Subject: Cake
18 February 06:38 GMT

Cuz –

OMG, what a night that was! Basically, I was going to sleep in the bathtub with the light on cos I'd had it listening to Ed's creepy horror story, but then I hear a knock on the door. I don't answer it, cos I think it's probably Bigstock. Or Bughole! But it's not, it's Bulmer and he's like, "I know how to help you so you don't get so scared!" So I go, "Oh yeah? How?" And he goes, "Cake."

So I tell him now is not the time to start thinking about food. And he says that's not what he meant. Then he explains that if I just *think* about something nice like cake, then I won't get scared.

I said that's not going to work. He said it will, if we both do it. Plus, I can't spend the night sleeping in the tub, cos then Bigstock will win. I said, you're mad at me, why are you helping me? He said we're friends. That's what friends do.

So all that made me feel pretty bad after what had happened earlier. But me and him go back in the room and Bigstock's like, "Great! You suckers are back for scary seconds! Excellent! Let me continue with your torture! So one night this writer guy is up in his office writing away, when he looks out of his window and he sees the demon Bughole standing over by some bushes in the garden..."

And that's when I say, "Eating cake?"

And Bigstock goes, "What?"

So I say, "Is Bughole eating cake?"

And Bigstock's like, "Bughole's a DEMON, you moron!!! Of course he's not eating CAKE!!! Demons don't eat cake!"

And that's when Bulmer said, "But he might like a cream sponge?"

Well, then me and Bulmer start laughing as we try to figure out what kind of cake this demon would like to eat before he starts stealing more kids. And as we go back and forth, even Kevin starts laughing and joining in too. And basically that was all it took before this scary story became a funny story that didn't scare me any more.

So then Bigstock says he's not going to bother telling us any more stories if we're going to make fun of them. And that was the last word we heard out of Ed. But you know what was really cool? I didn't even *think* about opening the door to let the light in, cos I fell asleep laughing.

I just hope this cake trick works on the Wall of Death today, cos I don't know how I'm going to abseil down a wall that's 100 feet high.

CHAPTER THIRTEEN
THE WALL OF DEATH

<u>Harry's Film Log</u>

Scene 12: Exterior. Zip wire. Day

So we're evens, going into the Last Challenge
and it's the SCARIEST one of all: The Wall of
Death! And Bulmer hates heights and so do I.
I think we might be spending tonight in the
woodshed.

U do the wall?
Charley

In tower now!
Harry

U going to do it?

I don't know!!!

It's easy.

If u r Bigstock. Or u. But
I'm not. OK. At top now!!!

206

Jessica straight out, no problem. Now Kevin.

OK. Bad news. Kevin and Georgia did it easy too! OMG, so now it's just me, Bigstock and Bulmer. If either me or Bulmer don't do it, then we've definitely lost!

Cuz – what happened?

U bail u little squirt?

Harry?

From Harry **to** Charley
Subject: Wall of Death
18 February 17:22 GMT

OMG, I did it!!!

From Charley **to** Harry
Subject: Wall of Death
18 February 10:28 MST

What do you mean you did it?

From Harry **to** Charley
Subject: Wall of Death
18 February 17:32 GMT

I abseiled 100 feet down from top to bottom!!!

From Charley **to** Harry
18 February 10:35 MST

I know, but how did u manage that?

_____

From Harry **to** Charley
18 February 17:50 GMT

I don't know. I guess after all that other outdoorsy
stuff we've been doing here for the last couple of
days and the thing with Bigstock and Bughole, I
thought what the hell. Maybe I should just give it a
try, and so what if I'm scared. Everybody is scared.
It's the Wall of Death!

So I get to the edge and Mr Forbes says, "Harry
– never thought I'd see you up here. Well done,
son!" Which was great. Until I had to walk

backwards over that ledge. Then I thought I can't do this. This is too scary! But Jessica is now down the bottom and she's like, "Come on, Harry – you can do this!" And with her and Bulmer's help, I just shut my eyes and went out the gate.

OMG scary! But then I was on the wall and I was like, "Oh my God, I *can* do this!" It was, like, *the* most incredible buzz!!! (Even better, BTW, than Aqualand!) And because I went out, Bulmer went out too. But you know what the really funny thing was? Bigstock. After all that mouthing off about how there was *nothing* in this camp that was going to frighten him cos he's the big man, he got to the top of the tower and FROZE. I mean, literally froze. Could not move. Bulmer got Bigstock on his camera phone saying, "Oh, I think I must have had too many pasties for lunch, cos I don't feel so good! Maybe I should sit down before I'm sick!" and then he climbed back down the ladders.

And this is a kid who told me and Bulmer that he climbed Mount Blanc with his dad when he was, like, eight. So you know what? He probably lied.

Georgia Gardener was not cool with him bailing and hasn't spoken to Bigstock since. So Bulmer still might be in with a chance for her.

Anyway, we WON the challenges (but not the cup, cos some other kids won that), which means *we* get to choose a dare for *them* to do. Yay!

Way to go, spud! So what's it gonna be?

CHAPTER FOURTEEN
CHICKEN DISCO

From Harry **to** Madonna
Subject: Bulmer
18 February 19:24 GMT

Dear Madonna, Queen of Pop, hi there!

My friend Bulmer really likes your music and
has chosen one of your great songs for the end
of camp disco – which is why I'm writing to you.
He needs your help, cos he wants to go out with
Georgia Gardener, but she's told my friend Jessica
that she thinks Ed Bigstock will ask her to go out
with him at the disco tonight. I told Bulmer if he
wants to go out with her, he's got to ask, cos she's
not a mind reader. But he says he won't do it, cos
Bigstock's the best-looking kid in our school, so
what chance has he got, cos he's kinda chubby.

I said Bigstock doesn't have what he's got, cos

he's *funny* and girls really like that. He said I
don't know what I'm talking about and he's
not gonna ask.

I know you are on this big world tour and you have
A LOT of important stuff to do, but can you write
him a short note about how he should always
chase his dreams? Or how girls prefer funny guys
to good-looking guys? (And, BTW, I don't mind

if you lie.) Then that would really help him, cos I think he might be in with a chance with Georgia, even if he doesn't.

Thanks a lot for reading this. Plz GBTM soon.

Good luck and have fun.

Harry Riddles

From Charley **to** Harry
Subject: Disco
18 February 14:03 MST

How was the disco?

From Harry **to** Charley
Subject: Disco
18 February 21:22 GMT

OMG FUNNY!

From Charley **to** Harry
18 February 14:25 MST

Did you get Bulmer to go?

From Harry **to** Charley
Subject: Chicken Disco
18 February 21:39 GMT

Yeah – but only after I said we should use the dare to make it as hard as possible for Bigstock to ask Georgia Gardener to go out with him. I said what we should do is make Bigstock wear fancy dress to the disco, cos Little Dave told me they have lots of funny things to choose from in the dressing-up room in the basement. So I take Bulmer and Jessica down there and you know what we found? Chicken suits! You should have seen Bigstock's face when Bulmer gave him one to wear. It was hilarious.

So Bigstock gets in his chicken suit and we give the other one to Kevin and we all go down to the disco and Bigstock's like, what about Georgia?

Where's her chicken suit? I tell him we have a different dare lined up for Georgia. And Bulmer's like, we do? And I tell him to relax, cos I've got it all figured out.

Anyway, we head over to the recreation room, which has now been turned into this super-cool night club and some of the guys who work at the camp have now got dressed up as bouncers with shorts and ties and shades. So when we walk past them, they start laughing and Bigstock and Kevin are like, maybe we'll just skip the disco and go and watch some TV. But Jessica tells them the dare was to wear the chicken suit *at* the disco, not in the TV room.

So we take the glo-sticks and the glo-necklaces and we walk into the room and it's all blacked out and has laser lights and a VIP area and I'm thinking if this is what discos are like, I like them. They even have a chill-out area to one side, where you could play pool, or giant Jenga, or do hoola hoops, or play skittles. It was incredible.

But nobody was dancing. So Little Dave and Mr Forbes get us all to do the conga, which kind of breaks the ice. But there's no sign of Georgia, so I go off to find her and she says she didn't want to come to the disco, cos she thought we were going to put her in a chicken suit. I said her dare is *not* wearing a chicken suit. Or looking stupid in any way. That's only for Bigstock.

So I bring her into the disco and Bulmer's waiting and I tell him this is your big moment. Ask her for a dance. But he's shy and he won't ask, which I knew would happen, cos he'd already told me he wasn't up for it. So I go over to Georgia and I tell her that her dare is to ask Bulmer for a dance.

So she goes over and asks him, and I look at him, and I think his face is going to split in two he looks so happy. But then Bigstock comes over and tells her if she's dancing with anybody, she's dancing with him. But Georgia just looks at him and says, chickens don't dance with girls, they dance with other chickens, and anyway, she wants to dance with BULMER!

Well me and Jessica are watching and we're thinking, OMG this is so great, but please, please don't mess this up, Bulmer! Be cool!

And you know what? We didn't need to worry. Bulmer is a sick dancer! Moonwalks, the splits, multiple spins – he even tried to spin on his head on the floor! He was the best kid out there.

Georgia said afterwards that this was her favourite
night *ever* and thank God we dared her to ask
Bulmer for a dance. Otherwise she would have
been stuck with a stupid chicken all night.

So all in all, A GREAT NIGHT!

From Charley **to** Harry
18 February 14:43 MST

Cool. So now what? Early bed and more scary stories from Ed?

From Harry **to** Charley
18 February 21:44 GMT

Nope. I've figured out how I can make it up to Jessica. I have a little surprise for her...

From Charley **to** Harry

18 February 14:46 MST

Yeah? What?

From Harry **to** Jessica
Subject: Midnight Feast
18 February 21:48 GMT

Dear Jessica,

Set your alarm for 11.40pm. We will meet on the
BACK STAIRS at 11.50pm. Remember to stay on
the left side of the hallway, where the floorboards
do not creak when you leave your dorm. If you
see a light on under Mr Forbes's door, do not freak
out. I think he falls asleep with the light on. BTW,
what food do you want?

Love,

Harry xxxxx

From Jessica **to** Harry
Subject: Midnight Feast
18 February 21:52 GMT

Dear Harry,

I think honey and sugar sandwiches! This is SO exciting!

Love,

Jessica xxx

BTW, Georgia Gardener wants to come with us, but she doesn't want Ed to come.

From Harry **to** Jessica
18 February 22:02 GMT

Dear Jessica,

I love honey and sugar sandwiches! But why
doesn't Georgia want Ed to come?
Love,

Harry xxx

From Jessica **to** Harry
18 February 22:06 GMT

Dear Harry,

She says she just wants Bulmer to come. She thinks
he's sweet and funny. Plus, he knows how to bust

some sick dance moves.

Love,

Jessica xxx

From Harry **to** Jessica
18 February 22:07 GMT

Dear Jessica,

I just told Bulmer what you told me. He said this is
the best holiday EVER. See you at 11.50. BTW, I'm
bringing the camera so we can film the feast.

Love,

Harry xxx

I have my alarm set but just on vibrate so Ed won't wake up. I'll wake you. OK?
Harry

Got it, but I can't sleep. I need to plan the menu!
Bulmer

What menu?

For Georgia.

There is no menu. It's a midnight feast. Honey and sugar sandwiches. That's it.

But I was thinking nachos. Hot chocolate. Cupcakes. Egg in a hole. Popcorn. Grilled cheese sandwich. Pancakes and syrup. Yorkshire Puddings. OMG, this could be so gr8! What do you think?

We're having sandwiches.

Got it. BTW, did I say this is going to be so gr8?

U did. And stop txting me. Bigstock's getting suspicious!

What's the surprise?

From Harry **to** Charley
Subject: Midnight Feast
18 February 23:01 GMT

A midnight feast!!! And we are now *ready*. The plan
is, we will all take empty glasses, so if we get caught
we can just say we were thirsty and needed a drink!
I went down into the kitchen after the disco and
made a list of stuff in the fridge that we can take
without anyone knowing it's gone. But basically
all we need is bread, butter, sugar and honey.

We will be taking lookouts. All mobile phones will be turned off. And we will wear socks, so we keep the noise down when we creep along the corridors!

Is there anything I have missed?

GBTM soon.

Harry

From Charley **to** Harry
Subject: Midnight Feasts
18 February 16:07 MST

Keep mobile phones ON – but leave them on VIBRATE only. If lookouts need to warn you of snooping teachers, you will need escape routes. Do you have any? If not, do a recce, locate some routes, then tell the others. Got it?

From Harry **to** Charley
18 February 23:08 GMT

It's a little late to be finding escape routes.

From Charley **to** Harry
18 February 16:09 MST

Cuz,

A good boy scout is ALWAYS prepared!

From Harry **to** Charley
18 February 23:11 GMT

Yeah, but I can't leave the room and scout the routes without making Ed suspicious! So this Boy Scout is gonna hafta go unprepared.

From Charley **to** Harry
18 February 16:26 MST

Well, don't say I didn't warn ya! BTW, if any of you kids get caught, make sure you don't snitch. Good luck and happy feasting!

Charley

R u awake?
Harry

Leaving now!
Jessica

Ed might be awake. He just faked a . I think he knows what's up.

Ask him.

OK. I asked him. Maybe he is asleep. If not, too bad. See u on the stairs. We have 2 go.

Where r u?

Mr Forbes is singing in his room!!!

Sneak past. He won't hear. He's pretty deaf, but hurry! 12 minutes to go!

OK. He's not singing, he's SNORING. We r on our way.

Coast clear?
Harry

CLEAR!
Kevin

Harry to 3 others

Meet in kitchen in 2 minutes!

We r in the kitchen, the feast is made and we r about to EAT!

Kevin to Harry

What was that noise?
Kevin

When the clock struck 12, it scared
Bulmer and he dropped the butter dish!
Harry

Stay where you are. I think Little
Dave on the stairs? I can hear
something!

That was loud! What just
happened? Is everybody OK?

Knocked over rubbish bin!

Forbes on way! Get out!
Get out! Get out!

Which way did he go?

He's heard you!!! He's on the stairs!!!
RUN!!!

Where he now?

I dunno. Where u?

On roof of kitchen!!! Where's
Bulmer?

Forbes is in the kitchen!
IN THE KITCHEN!

Who was that screaming?
Was that Jessica? Is she
OK?

What happened?
R u there?

CHAPTER SIXTEEN
WAR PATH

From Harry **to** Charley
Subject: Boy scouts
19 February 19:20 GMT

Cuz –

I'm in heaps of trouble and I don't know what to
do.

From Charley **to** Harry
Subject: Boy scouts
19 February 12:22 MST

You kids get caught?

From Harry **to** Charley
Subject: Boy scouts
19 February 19:24 GMT

Kind of.

_____

From Charley **to** Harry
19 February 12:30 MST

What happened?

_____

From Harry **to** Charley
19 February 19:32 GMT

OK, so basically we fell off the roof and Jessica broke her leg and now her mum is ON THE WAR PATH and wants to take her out of school cos she thinks Jessica has fallen in with a BAD crowd, and the camp was a SHAMBLES, and Mr Forbes is a useless headteacher who can't control or look after his students!!!

From Charley **to** Harry
19 February 12:34 MST

Well that kinda sucks.

From Harry **to** Mrs MacDougal
Subject: Jessica
19 February 20:14 GMT

Dear Mrs MacDougal,

Please don't blame Mr Forbes, or my school, or
Little Dave for Jessica's accident. It was my fault.
I thought a midnight feast would be a really fun
thing for us to do after we'd finished our course.

My cousin told me if we were
good boy scouts, we would
have scouted some
emergency exit routes
before the feast, in case
we got found out. But
I didn't check for escape
routes, cos I hadn't thought

about it. But if I had, we probably would never have got trapped up on the kitchen roof, or fallen down those drainpipes when Mr Forbes came in the kitchen. We didn't know they weren't screwed into the wall. That's why we fell in the pond. I'm sorry Jessica got hurt.

Does she really have to move schools? How about if I move school? Would that make any difference?

Harry

How's your leg?
Harry

Hurts. But I'm OK. U?
Jessica

Is yr mum really gonna make u do this?

She said with friends like mine, who needs enemies?

From Harry **to** Little Dave
Subject: Mrs MacDougal
21 February 19:22 GMT

Hi Little Dave,

I'm back home now, but my dad said I should write to you and apologise in case you got in trouble with Jessica's mum because of what happened to Jessica. So here it is.

S O O O O O R R R R R R R R Y ! ! ! ! ! !

And BTW, thanks for everything. Maybe see you again one day.

Good luck and have fun.

Harry

From Little Dave **to** Harry
Subject: Jessica
21 February 21:30 GMT

Hi Harry,

Thanks for writing and don't worry about Jessica's mum. How is Jessica anyway? Are you guys back at school? Did you finish the film? When can I see it?

You take care of yourself and be good (and if you can't be good, please don't fall off any more roofs)!

Little Dave

BTW, thanks for the tips. I can now rake train and I have got to LEVEL 2. Awesome, right?

From Harry **to** Little Dave
Subject: Jessica
22 February 19:33 GMT

Hi Little Dave,

Jessica has her leg in a cast and is getting better, but her mum wants her to move schools at the end of this term. I'm going to edit the film this week and when it's done I'll put it up on Dropbox and send you a link.

Thanks again for looking after us.

Harry

Little Man, Mum showed me your movie. It's great. She also told me Jessica will be leaving your school at the end of term. Are you OK about that?
Dad

No.
Harry

Then we should talk when I get home, cos I have an idea that might help.

OK.

See you tomorrow.

CHAPTER SEVENTEEN
TEAM PLAYER

From Harry **to** Little Dave
Subject: Team Player
1 March 18:43 GMT

Hi Little Dave,

Good news (maybe). Me and my dad took all the
footage I had taken of our time at camp and we
sat up in my bedroom and recut the story, so it
became a film about Jessica and her time at camp.

When it was done, my dad took me over to
Jessica's house and when her mum finally
answered the door, he asked if I could show
her the movie I'd made. I don't think she was
interested, cos she was still mad with me, but my
dad made her.

So we went into the house and I put my laptop on

the kitchen table and I played her the movie.

I had some really cool stuff in it. You remember when Ed nearly made Georgia cry after they lost at archery? And then Jessica ran in to make her feel better and Georgia was like, "Jessica, you're the best friend ever!" Plus, all that stuff of Jessica laughing and having a good time – you know, like at quad-biking? Or when in the bus after kayaking, she got everybody singing a Monkees song to make Bulmer feel better and he said that she's the greatest? Or on the beach when we rolled all the way down the sand dunes to the bottom, when Ed had gone off to the minibus after surfing? Or how she showed no fear on the Wall of Death and had everybody at the bottom cheering, and clapping, and whooping for her?

Well, when Mrs MacDougal saw that, I think she

started to realise that Jessica has a lot of good friends at my school, and the teachers and camp leaders aren't so bad either.

Then she said that maybe she should reconsider her decision, and she thanked me for showing her the movie. After that, she kicked us out, cos she had to go feed Thunderbolt (that's her horse). So fingers crossed, Jessica won't be leaving.

And BTW, you won't believe what else happened. You know I had that one v one death match that I was going to play against darkassassin300? Turns out, the kid didn't make it online that night. So now I have the rematch next week. And I got a feeling that the one thing that he said was always missing from my game – how to be a team player – won't be missing after my time at camp. So thanks for everything. It really was the best holiday ever.

Good luck and have fun.

Harry